JUST ONE CHRISTMAS

A Green Mountain Valley Romance

MICHELLE WINDSOR

This one's for you DeDe…

Chapter One

"Bex?"

My breath catches in my throat, my heart skidding to a halt as I realize the single moment I've been dreading more than any other is finally happening. There's only one person who has ever called me Bex. I want to drop the jar of jam I'm holding and bolt for the exit, but I keep my feet planted and lift my head, my eyes immediately locking with his dark green irises. Yep, he's still just as gorgeous as I remember. And holy shit, when did he become a man? I take in the dark stubble lining his chiseled chin, framing lips that don't require any further call to attention, but damn it, seem to sure have captured mine.

"I didn't realize you were in town." His statement comes out more like a question, which I choose to ignore, since it seems rather obvious what the answer is.

I shift my focus back to his eyes, remembering that those lips were the reason we haven't spoken in almost five years.

"Maxwell." I purse my mouth in a thin line, realizing how angry I still am after saying his name out loud for the first time in so long.

He grimaces. "You know I hate when people call me that."

I keep silent, refusing to call him anything he might like. He clears his throat, shuffling his feet back and forth, then speaks again. "Blackberry always was your favorite."

My forehead creases as I stare back at him, frowning in confusion.

He nods and glances down at my hands. Oh shit. The jam. I completely forgot I was holding it. It may have had something to do with the way the timber of his voice seemed to still have a way of reaching into the depths of my soul, caressing it into submission. Wait, what? I shake my head, disgusted at myself for feeling anything else than hatred for this boy. Okay, he's a man now; a really hot man. But whatever, that's beside the point. He broke my heart into a million pieces, and that's what I need to remember right now.

"You want to talk to me about jam?" My question coming out on a sneer. "Are you kidding me?"

"Bex," he begins, but I cut him off, throwing my palm up flat in front of his face.

"Do not call me that."

His chin points north as he blows out a small breath and then lowers as he takes a tentative step closer to me. I counter by taking a step back. He frowns, small crinkles forming at the corners of his eyes, and for the first time I notice he looks tired. Before I can take the thought further, he speaks again. "Be-, Rebecca, if you would just sit down with me, I could explain what happened. Don't you think enough time has passed?"

I feel my cheeks flush from a surge of anger, my teeth gritting together as I seethe back at him. "I know what happened, Maxwell." I practically spit venom when I say his name again, making it clear how much it despises me. "I saw it with my own two eyes. I don't think I need to rehash it."

"It's not what it looked like." He rakes a hand through his brown locks. "I would never do anything to hurt you like that."

For a moment, I almost believe him. But when I close my eyes to blink, all I can see is his hand cupped around the cheek of my best friend, their lips pressed together under a sprig of mistletoe. On the night I thought he was going to propose to me. "But you did, Max." I blink repeatedly to keep the tears threatening to fall at bay and continue in a whisper. "You shattered me."

His face contorts as if he's in pain and he moves toward me, his arms opening to embrace me, but I wave my arms, backing away. I spin around, absently setting the jam down on a random shelf before fleeing from the store, and from the heartache I thought I was over.

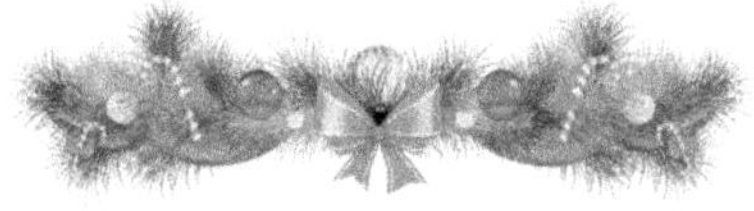

Three hours later, I'm curled up on the couch under a fluffy blanket, my little Yorkie snuggled in my lap as I stare absently at the flames flickering in the fireplace. I wish my mom was still here because she would know exactly what to say to make me feel better. Or at least what I should do when it comes to Max. I somehow managed to avoid him for the better part of five years, and truly believed that enough time had passed that when I did see him again, he would have no effect on me at all. So much for wishful thinking.

But, I guess I shouldn't be surprised that I ran into him. There are less than a thousand people living in Green Mountain Valley. It's the kind of place where everyone knows everyone, and also everyone else's business. Even if I hadn't come face to face with him today, I'm sure someone would have shared the news that I was in town. I reach toward the side table for my wine, but freeze in place when I hear a knock at the door.

Before I can even think about who it might be, the ball of fur that was sleeping so soundly just a second ago, darts out of my lap, charging toward the foyer, barking at the top of his little lungs. I throw the blanket off myself as I rise, chasing after him, scooping him up as I pull the door open. "Quiet, you little monster."

"Is that who was making all that noise?"

For the second time today, my heart beat stalls, my head snapping up. "What are you doing here?"

"Well, I do live right next door." He shrugs, one side of his mouth quirking up in a hesitant smile.

I twist my head as I peer out the door, noting the Christmas lights brightening the porch of the house a few thousand yards away. I arch one brow as I turn back to him. "You're still living at your parent's house?"

"It's mine now." He extends his fingers just under the dog's nose to let him sniff and then lowers them to scratch under his chin. "What's this guy's name?"

"Hercules." I frown, looking down at the dog and then back toward the house. "What do you mean it's yours now?"

"Well, if that's not the definition of ironic, I'm not sure what is." He chuckles, a grin lighting up his face, and I hate my pulse races just the slightest as I note again how much more attractive he's become with age.

"Will you stop changing the subject?" I counter, an edge to my voice caused by my own confusion. "You always do that."

"I thought we were talking about your dog." He leans against the doorjamb, looking over my shoulder into the house. I know he wants me to ask him in, but that is not happening. No way. No how.

"I was talking about your parent's house." I roll my eyes. "Never mind." I let out a huff. "Why are you here again?"

"I brought you this." It's then, as he's raising his arm, that I see he's carrying a basket. I take in the contents as he holds it out to me, my mouth falling open but silent as he continues. "I didn't mean to scare you out of the market earlier."

I gape at his offering another minute before logic clicks into place and realize now I have to let him in. Well, shit. Score one for Maxwell.

"I think this is everything you need?" I tear my gaze

away to look up at him as he keeps speaking. "I was kind of guessing, or maybe hoping, that you were getting what you needed to make your famous jam cookies."

I nod, still too dumbstruck to form any witty remarks, and then step back, pushing the door open wider, motioning with my chin for him to come in. He does, closing the door behind him once he's inside, watching as I lower the dog to the floor. Hercules spins in a circle before scurrying over to Max, his nails clicking against the hardwood of the floor as he sniffs every inch of his boots.

"He's cute." He offers me the basket again, and this time, now that my hands are free, I take it. "But why not just get a cat if you wanted something that small?"

"Because cats are assholes with attitude." I snap. I look down at the dog, still sniffing away, and smile warmly. "And Hercules is always happy to see me and is extremely loyal."

"So, are you here all alone?" He asks, ignoring my jab at his infidelity.

I grip the basket tighter and pull it against my waist as I turn my attention back to him. "No." I nod toward the dog. "I have Hercules."

"So we've established." He bends suddenly and swoops Hercules up, holding him against his chest as he stands, swinging his eyes to lock with mine. "Are you a single parent? Or is there a dad around somewhere for Hercules?"

My brows crease as my eyes slant. "Is this your way of asking if I'm married?"

"No, I know you aren't. I talk to Jonny a couple times a year. But, it was my way of asking if there was a boyfriend floating around here. I thought it might be why you were hesitant to let me in."

"First, you know damn well why I don't want you in my house. I think I made that pretty clear earlier today." I plant my foot and spin away from him to storm toward the kitchen, spouting over my shoulder as I go. "And second, it's none of your damn business if I have a boyfriend." I slam the basket down on the island, spinning around to continue and end up almost banging into his chest. "Christ, Maxwell, a little space please!"

He takes an abrupt step back, raising his hands in the air defensively. He must have put the dog down somewhere along the way because he's no longer holding him. I throw a fist on my hip, jutting it out. "And how come I didn't know you still talked to Jonny? He never mentioned it."

"Probably because he's afraid he'd get shot for consorting with the enemy." Max mumbles under his breath, his tone changing completely when he sees my expression harden. "I'm just saying Bex, Jonny and I have been best friends our whole lives. Of course we're still going to talk."

"But he's my brother." I point a finger to my chest. "Mine." I throw my hands up in the air. "Doesn't anyone have any loyalty to me around here?"

"Hey, I was always loyal to you, Bex." He defends.

"Yeah, until you weren't." I chuff back, crossing my arms.

"That's not fair." He takes a step closer to me, his voice lowering. "Especially since you haven't let me tell you my side of the story."

"No." I close my eyes and shake my head, opening them as I sigh. "I've had enough today. I knew coming back here was going to be hard, but because of them. Not because of you too." I unfold my arms, letting them hang by my sides as I look down at my stockinged feet. "I wanted just one Christmas where I wasn't sad anymore." I drag my gaze up, one corner of my mouth tilted into a frown. "I thought maybe enough time had passed."

"I get it." His hand reaches up to cup my cheek gently. "I'm sorry. I'm not trying to make things more difficult for you."

It's hard. So hard not to take comfort in his touch. So many wonderful memories flood back when I feel the warmth of his skin against mine. I want so badly to rest my head against his chest and let him hold me. But I don't. Because all I can see when I close my eyes is his hand against her cheek, regardless of the fact that he's here, touching me now. Instead, I pull away from his hold and walk past him to the front door.

I hear him let out a deep breath and then his footsteps a second later as he follows me. I grip the handle of the door to pull it open. "Thank you for the basket. It really was thoughtful."

"You don't have a Christmas tree yet." He looks in the fireplace's direction, where normally, we'd have a ten-foot tree by now.

"Dad always got the tree." I whisper, staring at the blank space in the living room, before forcing a small smile as I turn back to Max. "I've still got time. Christmas isn't for another ten days."

Before I can react, he leans over and plants a kiss against the top of my head. "Good night, Bex."

He strides out the door and down the porch steps, my quiet response carried into the night by the wind. "Good night, Max."

Chapter Two

"Ouch!" I jerk my arm out of the oven, making sure I don't drop the tray of cookies in my gloved hand until it's over the counter. I rush over to the sink and flip the faucet on cold. I pull the oven mitt off my hand and then hold my burnt arm underneath the running water. A dark red splotch glares back at me and I pray it won't turn into a blister. It's the second time today I've burnt myself making these damn cookies. It has been awhile since I baked, but I didn't expect to have battle wounds from my efforts.

Thank goodness that was the last batch. I glance around the kitchen, taking in all the damn cookies I baked today, and can't contain the giggle that bubbles up. There has to be over a hundred cookies. Who the hell is going to eat all these? As if on cue, a loud knock sounds from the front door, Hercules bursting into guard duty from the living room barking fiercely. I shut the water off, grab a dish towel, and press it against my burn as I make my way to the foyer.

"Hercules, quiet down!" I command. Not that it does any good. He stops long enough to turn his head toward me, but then just continues on with his warning to my would be assailant. I scoot him away from the door with my foot and pull the door open.

"Don't need a doorbell with that guy around, huh?"

I swing my head up, my eyes popping wide for just a second before I reign in my surprise. "Did you forget something last night?"

"Nope." He leans inside the house inhaling. "Are those cookies I smell?" A wide grin breaks across his face as he turns to me. "Did you make the jelly ones?"

His smile seems to dull the fact that I'm supposed to hate him and I find myself grinning back as I nod. "Yep, I put your gift basket to good use."

"I sure hope you're planning to share." He bends down to scratch the fur on the top of Hercules' head, greeting him, before rising in front of me again.

"I made tons so you better take some or I'll be leaving the Valley ten pounds heavier than when I got here!" I joke, the smile freezing on my face when I notice his gaze traveling down the length of my body.

"I don't think ten or even twenty pounds could take away from your beauty, Bex." His eyes lock with mine, a flush of goosebumps breaking across my skin as my pulse shifts into a higher gear.

My cheeks heat and I know I'm blushing, which just pisses me off, because damn it, I promised myself I wouldn't fall prey to his charms. I wipe the smile from my lips, replacing it with a firm line. "Is there a reason for this uninvited intrusion, Maxwell?"

"Jesus, you're a tough nut to crack." He chuckles, running a hand over his stubbled jaw, his coy grin staying in place. He turns his body, sweeping his arm out toward the driveway. I shift my gaze in the direction he's pointing, as he announces the reason for his visit. "I brought you a tree."

My mouth falls open, my hand rising to cover it, as I take in the sight of the dark, green spruce strapped to the back of his truck. Five different emotions swirl through my head at once leaving me unsure how to respond. He brought me a tree? The tree and the outside lights were always my father's job, and he reveled in the responsibility of it. My mom and I did all the shopping, baking, present wrapping and decorating of the house for the holidays. My dad would joke that he needed to do something useful so my mom wouldn't replace him. I planned on waiting for Jonny to arrive with Natalie and the kids to get the tree. I was assuming my brother would take up the tradition.

"You look mad." He places both his hands on my upper arms to gently push me back far enough so he can shut the door behind us both. "Are you mad? Don't be mad. I just wanted to try to make you happy. Especially after what you said last night about being sad. I thought this might help."

I watch as he drags the hat he's wearing off his head, his dark brown hair sticking up in a thousand directions, and I finally react, laughter bursting from my chest. "You look like you stuck your finger in a light socket." I toss the towel onto the nearby side table, then reach up, standing on my tiptoes, to smooth down his unruly locks. My fingers brush through the thick strands, trying to groom them back into a tamed state, stilling when I feel his hands fall around my waist. I lower my eyes, locking onto green irises staring back at me with a look I remember well.

"This is the first time you've touched me in five years." He whispers, his breath warm as it feathers against my skin, diverting my gaze from his eyes to his lips. His perfect, puffy lips. His grip tightens, his fingertips digging into my soft flesh through the flannel shirt I'm wearing. My eyes dart up to his again, the irises darker than they were just a single glance ago. If I don't do something, I know he'll kiss me.

The awful thing is, I think I want him to. I can still remember what his lips felt like when they would meet mine; hot, and wet, and oh, the sweet taste of him. I miss that taste so much. I tilt my head up further and lean into him, my hands sliding through his hair to the back of his neck, a small gasp escaping as I'm shoved back, the loss of Max's grip on my waist, sudden and cold. Before I can even react, he flings the door open and is standing back on the porch. "I'm just going to go get the tree and bring it up on the porch so the branches can settle."

I can feel my mouth hanging open, my brow furrowing once again, as he strides off the porch and down to his truck. What the hell did I almost just do? Shit! Thank goodness one of us came to our senses! I continue watching him as he releases the straps holding the tree, crossing my arms over my chest to ward off some of the cold. He lifts it easily off the back of the truck, holding it over his head, reminding me again how much of a man he's become since our time together. He avoids eye contact as he props the tree in the porch's corner and fumbles with it a minute to make sure it's not going to topple over.

He turns and skips back down the steps, still not looking at me. "I'll come back later to help you put it in the stand."

"Wait." I call out, unfolding my arms as I walk to the top of the steps. "What about the cookies? Don't you want some?"

"I'll grab some later." He opens his truck door, tossing a wave as he climbs in, shouting his response. "See ya."

I cross my arms again, shaking my head as I watch him practically do a one-eighty out of the driveway he backs out so quickly. "See ya." I mumble, as I turn and go back into the house.

Anger claws in my gut as I scrub my face, change into my favorite pair of flannel pajamas, and crawl into bed next to Hercules. And it's not because I spent two hours digging through the garage to find the tree stand, the lights, and all the Christmas decorations to prep for Max to return, only to have him not show up. I'm pissed at myself for being disappointed he didn't come back over. Pissed that I forgot I wasn't supposed to like him anymore, or look forward to seeing him. And I certainly wasn't supposed to shower beforehand, putting on cute jeans, my favorite sweater and makeup.

"Stupid!" I burst out, punching balled fists into the surrounding covers, causing Hercules to yip in surprise and hop onto my chest. I lower my voice and unclench one hand to stroke his back. "I'm sorry, sweet boy. I didn't mean to scare you." I turn onto my side, Hercules readjusting himself in a snug ball up against my middle. I pat him gently, a soft snore sounding from him within moments, soothing my frustration away long enough for me to fall into a sound sleep not long after.

I blink awake, strips of sunlight peeking through the slots of the blinds covering my windows, brightening the room just enough to see. I stretch, rolling over onto my side, a yelp of surprise sounding from me as I jolt back, startling the long form lying next to me from his sound slumber. "Jesus Christ, Maxwell!" I sit up, pulling the covers over my chest. "What the hell are you doing in my bed?"

One corner of his mouth quirks into a tired smile as he shifts into a sitting position against the headboard, one hand ruffling through his messy locks. "Good morning to you too, Bex."

"Don't good morning me!" I throw a stern look down at Hercules, who is still curled in a tight ball against the warmth of Max's body. "And you, some guard dog you've turned out to be!"

"He's five pounds. Did you really think he'd be much of a threat?" Max yawns, drawing my attention to his lips. His puffier than usual lips that he just wiped his tongue across, leaving them shiny. I snap my lids shut and shake my head. No! I do not like Maxwell Chastain. No matter how good his lips look; shiny and wet and begging to be kissed.

I blow out a breath, open my eyes and try again. "How did you get into my house and what on earth are you doing in my bed?"

"I've lived next door to you my entire life. You don't think I know where you hide the key?" He chuckles and I watch as he slides out of the bed, stretching his hands above his head, the hem of his t-shirt rising just enough to give me a tiny glimpse of bare skin at his waist.

I want to kill myself as a pulse of need between my legs causes my panties to dampen. He lowers his arms, his body turning toward the bed, then stills when he looks directly at me. I realize my mouth is hanging open, so I slam it shut, then jump out of bed, turning my back to him so he can't see the flush of embarrassment blooming across my cheeks. I huff, shoving my feet into my slippers, feigning more anger than I really feel. "That doesn't give you the right to just come in anytime you want. And it especially doesn't mean you can come into my bed!"

I twirl around and smack right into his hard torso. His hands are immediately around my arms, holding me in place so I don't fall backwards. "Christ!" I glare up at him. "Will you stop sneaking up on me like that!"

"I forgot that you're pretty cranky in the morning." Another cocky smile tugs those lips up, his grip releasing me as he steps back. "You want some coffee?" He strolls toward the door. "I could use some coffee." He pulls it open and walks out into the hallway and starts down the stairs.

"Let's go make some coffee." He calls over his shoulder, not waiting for me to respond or follow.

But follow I do, exactly ten seconds after him. The exact time it takes for me to gather my senses and remember that he's in my house. That I'm the boss here, not him! I burst into the kitchen, full of fire and ready for battle, all anger extinguishing when I see him filling a coffeepot with water, humming 'Dreaming of a White Christmas' to himself. A flashback of my father doing the exact same thing, humming that exact same song, rolls over me like a freight engine.

"My dad used to hum that whenever he was in the kitchen." I muse out loud.

"I remember." He pours the water into the coffeemaker, fills a liner with coffee, then turns the button on to brew the pot. "Your dad loved Christmas."

"Yeah." I nod, a small smile forming at the memory. "I miss them." I pull a stool from the breakfast bar and sit down.

"I think he's going to get his wish this year." He continues, leaning on the counter across from me, his arms stretched out in front of him.

"What's that?" My head tilts.

"A white Christmas." He pulls his phone out of his pocket and touches the screen, reading it, then nodding. "Yep, they're predicting eighteen to twenty inches on Friday."

"Great." I mumble. "Can't wait to do all that shoveling on my own."

"I'll come help." He offers, pushing himself off the counter, turning around to open a cabinet before pulling two mugs out. Like he lives here or something. Which reminds me, he still hasn't told me what he was doing in my bed last night.

"How about you explain how you ended up in my bed first?" I drum the counter with my fingernails.

"Ah. Didn't forget about that I see?" He's silent a moment while he pours coffee into both mugs, leaving his black, and opening the fridge to grab my flavored creamer before adding just the right amount. How the hell does he still remember how I like my coffee?

He slides the mug across the counter to me, and remains leaning over it, his gaze swinging up to mine. "Well, I felt bad about not showing up last night." He blows on the edge of the cup, then takes a gulp of the dark liquid before continuing. "The Clancy's barn went up last night. They called in all the guys. It was crazy until after one, otherwise I would have tried to call to let you know."

"Oh, no." I sit up straighter, my hands wrapping around the mug for warmth. "Was it a total loss?"

"Yeah." He frowns. "We got most of the sheep out, but they lost their two horses, and they think a couple cats."

"That sucks." My expression matches his. "Can we do anything for them? Should we go over there today?"

"Don't think there's much we can do. The fire investigator will go out today to narrow down the cause. Pretty sure the Lemieux's were going to let them keep the sheep in their barn for now. They've got the extra room."

"Poor Mike and Melanie." I take a sip of my coffee.

"Yep." He nods, his hand scraping down the scruff lining his face. "So, anyway, I thought maybe you might still be up.

Wasn't sure how late your clock was now that you're a city girl and all." He chuckles, his eyes twinkling as he glances over at me. "I let myself in, took my boots off and went up to your room."

He turns and refills his cup, holding the pot up to see if I want anymore. I shake my head. "And? You ended up in my bed, how?" I push.

"I saw you lying there, curled up like a kitten, just like years ago." He gives me a small smile. "Remember all the times I would sneak out of Jonny's room to see you? How we would end up talking half the night about everything under the sun until the sun came up?"

I stare down into my cup, afraid if I look into his eyes, he'll know exactly how much I've thought about those times over the years. I nod but say nothing.

"Well, when I saw you last night, being in your room again after so long, it just felt so much like being home. I was only going to lie down for five minutes. I swear." He shrugs, taking another gulp. "Guess I was more tired than I realized."

What could I say to that? I suppose I should be angry, but how could I be? Being around him, especially in this house, felt like home. It felt like everything was normal again. Like nothing bad had ever happened. Instead, I just nodded and simply said, "Okay."

We drink our coffee in silence for the next few minutes. I think both of us unsure what to say next until Max finally pushes back from the counter and stands tall. "I'm on at noon for a forty-eight, so I wanted to get that tree in the house and in the stand for you before I have to go in."

"You were up half the night fighting a fire, and you have to go back in four hours, to work the next forty-eight and you're worried about my tree?"

"Well, ya." He gives me a broad smile that lights up his entire face. "I told you I would."

I laugh in disbelief as I climb off my stool. "You're too much."

"Better than not enough." He says, his voice serious, his eyes locking with mine just long enough to send a shiver down my spine, before he nods again and strides out of the kitchen toward the living room.

Chapter Three

I pull into the driveway, my brows furrowing as I register a man on a ladder leaning against the side of my house. I shut the car off and open the door, climbing out to get a better look so I can see who it might be. The man turns and waves, a smile stretching across my face as realization dawns.

"Mr. Chastain!" I wave as I walk closer. "What in the world are you doing up there?"

"Had to get these lights up before the snow comes in." He steps down the ladder until he's finally on the ground beside me. "And I think it's fine time you started calling me Bill. You may have outgrown Mr. Chastain by now."

I don't have time to object because a second later, his strong arms enfold me in a tight hug. "How are you, my girl?" His voice is muffled against my hat, but it doesn't block the sincerity and warmth from his question. I wrap my arms around his waist and squeeze back just as hard. Max's mom and dad were like second parents growing up. I didn't realize just how much I missed either of them until this moment.

"I miss you." We pull back from each other, his eyes a little misty as a warm smile lifts his mouth.

"We miss you too." He looks up at the sky, then back at me. "All of you."

"Stop or you'll have me in tears." I say through a forced smile, motioning toward the house. "You don't have to hang up the lights. I'm sure Jonny will do it when he gets here."

"Nonsense." He waves me off. "They need to get up before the storm comes in. No way Jonny will be able to hang 'em up with two feet of snow on the roof. Besides, since I've retired, I'm bored as hell! If I don't do this, Denise will have me frosting cookies or something silly like that."

I laugh. "Well, we can't have that now, can we?"

"I know Max would be over here doing it if he wasn't on shift right now, and anyway, it's what your dad would want."

I nod, knowing it's true, wishing that it wasn't. "You sure you should be up on that ladder with no help out here?"

"I spent thirty years going up and down them working fires. I think I can handle this." He chuckles as looks toward the car. "You need help to bring anything in?"

"No, I got it. It's only a couple of bags." I open my arms, stepping into him to give him another hug. "Thank you for this."

"No thank you needed." He pecks my cheek as he releases me, turning to move back to his task, talking over his shoulder. "You better go over and see Denise too. She's been trying to give you your space, but she's been itching for a visit."

"Yes, sir." I smile, feeling genuinely content. "I'll go over after I put away the groceries."

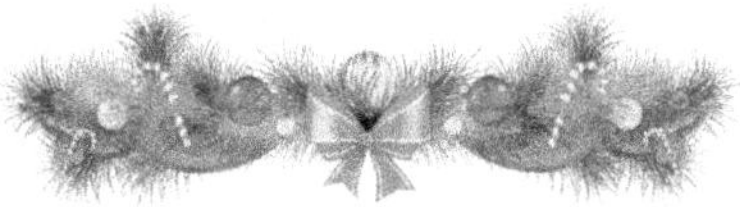

Thirty minutes later, I lift my hand to knock on the Chastain's front door, but it flies open before I can make contact, startling me.

"It sure took you long enough!" Mrs. Chastain, Denise, gives me a stern look, then winks, a grin lighting up her face as she draws me into her arms. "I've been waiting to do this for four days."

"I'm sorry I didn't come over sooner." I begin when she steps back to pull me into the house. "I just-"

"It's okay." She interrupts me. "No apologies." She takes my coat and hangs it on a hook and then links an arm with mine to guide me through the entryway into the kitchen. "You have nothing to apologize for. I can only imagine how hard this must be for you. Sit." She pats my hand as she releases me, pointing to a stool. "You want coffee?" She raises a brow, a little smirk lifting one corner of her mouth. "Or I have wine?"

"Definitely wine." I sit on the stool, grinning. I watch her open a bottle and pull two glasses from a rack, filling each. She moves to sit next to me, placing a glass in front of me.

"So, tell me. How are you doing over there? It surprised me when Max said you were all by yourself." Her hand moves to cover one of mine, her touch warm and comforting.

"I'm okay." I take a small sip of the wine, my lips turning down into a frown. "It's weird though. I know they're gone, but being in the house makes it feel like they aren't. Sometimes I think I smell Dad's aftershave when I walk into the bathroom. Or I'll go into the living room and I swear I can see Mom curled up in her chair reading a book." I look up, shrugging. "Of course, she's not there. Neither one of them are. I can feel them though. Little pieces of them are scattered all over the place."

"Does it make you feel happy or sad?" Her hand still wrapped around mine.

"I don't know." I shrug again. "It's bittersweet, I guess. I know I'll never get to talk to them again, but I take comfort in feeling them around me. I wasn't sure what I was going to feel. I haven't been in the house since the funeral. But it's been better than I thought."

"Well, I'm glad you're here, and that we were here as well." She squeezes my fingers before releasing them to take a drink. "Bill and I got in the day before you."

"Were you away?"

"We live in Florida now. Official snowbirds." Her brow creases. "Didn't Max tell you?"

"I mean, he mentioned something about the house being his now, but I was so flustered after not talking to him for so long that we somehow never got back around to it."

"Wait, you two haven't been talking?" She sits up straighter, concern etched on her face.

"The other day was the first time I spoke to Max in almost five years." I swallow hard. "I hadn't spoken to him since I caught him kissing Stacy. And when he didn't speak to me at the funeral, I just assumed he wanted to keep it that way."

"Oh, honey." Her palm raises and lands over her heart. "Do you really not know?"

"Know what?" I lean forward, my breath stuck somewhere in my chest as I wait for her to continue.

"I can't believe you don't know this." She grimaces, shaking her head, then continues. "He was first on the scene of your parent's accident." I reel back at her words, her hand finding mine again, clasping it tight. "He had been in Burlington that afternoon to watch UVM's homecoming game. He was on his way home when he found them. The moose was on the hood of the car, so he said he didn't know it was them at first. Not until he tried to pry one door open and saw who was inside the car."

"Oh my God." I feel a trickle slide down my cheek, but do nothing to wipe it away. "I had no idea."

"He called the station, telling them to send an ambulance and rescue. When they got there, they found him trying to drag the moose off the car." She closes her eyes, her lips pursing into a tight line. She blinks a few times and then continues. "Of course, you know a moose weighs well over a thousand pounds. They said his hands were raw and bleeding from the broken glass of the windshield, his clothing covered in blood from the moose, but he wouldn't stop. He tried so hard to get to them."

I blink, my lashes thick with tears, my voice trembling as I speak. "How come no one ever told me this? How come you didn't mention it at the funeral?"

"I don't know, honey." Her eyes finding mine. "I thought you knew." This time, both her hands wrap around mine. "But I'm sure that's why he didn't speak to you at the funeral. He was distraught for weeks. Maybe even months. He carried so much guilt over not being able to save them. Not because he didn't care for you, or want to talk to you. I don't think he would have been able to without breaking down, and he knew that wasn't what you needed from him then."

"But the coroner's report stated they both died on impact. There was nothing Max could have done."

"I know that. And you know that. But it took a long time for Max to realize that." She releases my hands to reach for her glass, taking a hearty sip. "He's okay now. The department set him up with an amazing counselor."

I wipe my cheeks, patting my hands on my jeans to dry them, then stare up at her. "I still can't believe I didn't know he found them. Jonny never said anything to me either."

"I don't know what to tell you, dear. I don't think it was intentional." Her mouth lifts into a smile, but sadness still shines from her eyes. "Just know that losing your parents may have been as hard on him as it was for you. He loved them very much."

"I know he did." I whisper, clasping my hands in my lap.

"And I'll tell you something else." The tone of her voice becomes sharp, demanding my attention, my brows shooting up as I look at her. "That boy never had feelings for anyone but you and absolutely did not have any for Stacy. You need to put your pride aside and have a conversation with him about that, once and for all young lady."

I break eye contact, bowing my head as my body sags in defeat, mumbling. "I know, I know."

We spend the next two hours drinking wine and talking, my heart full for the first time in so long. We share childhood memories, town gossip, and more laughter than I can remember in years. It's in the middle of a story about how Max and I snuck out one night with a stolen bottle of wine that Bill enters the house, calling out to us.

"Can I interest anyone in a little light display?" We both rise and make our way to the front door. Bill's rosy cheeks lift in a smile when he spots us. "You want to come see the lights? I'm all done."

"Absolutely!" I exclaim, genuine excitement bubbling up. We bundle up in our coats and head back over to my house. I can see the lights glowing from the Chastain's, and I'm already in awe. The closer we get, the brighter they shine, and the fuller my heart feels. I whip my head in his direction. "You even did the tree?" There is a fifty-foot pine tree that's always stood between our houses. Bill and my dad always argued about whose property the tree was actually on. My dad claimed it officially when I was four and began decorating it, and every year thereafter.

"Of course! Your dad would have haunted me if I didn't!" His smile growing wider.

We all stop when we reach the front of the house, our faces glowing, reflections of the colors shimmering in the darkness. "It's so beautiful." I murmur, admiring the simple splendor of the lights, the spirit of the holiday finally seeping into my mourning soul, thawing away my grief.

Chapter Four

I wake the next day knowing what I need to do, even though I know it won't be easy. It was time for me to put my hurt pride aside and give Max the opportunity to explain what happened between him and Stacy. I get up, take a quick shower, dress and take Hercules for a quick walk. I pack up more than half the cookies I made and then drive to the fire station. It's just a little past eight, which I know is a bit early, but I'm hoping I'll catch him between calls. I know he's only on until noon, but I couldn't push aside the sense of urgency I felt to talk to him.

It had been years since I stepped into the station, and then it was always to visit Max's dad, or drop off food Mrs. Chastain had made for the crew. My stomach clenches in a tight knot, my heart racing as I walk through the large bays where all the trucks are parked. I hear voices, so move in that direction. I pause when I reach the doorway to the kitchen, scanning the room full of people eating breakfast, until I find who I'm looking for. Our eyes lock, a smile lifting to expose his dimples as he rises from the chair he's sitting in.

"Bex!" He strides in my direction, all the other occupants in the room turning their attention to me. "What are you doing here?"

"I brought these for everyone." I thrust the container I'm holding into his hands, my face heating as all eyes focus on me. "I hope everyone likes blackberry jam cookies."

He turns, depositing the cookies on the table, hands immediately lifting the lid to sample the goods. I smile, my heart finally slowing to a normal beat, when people reach in for a second and third cookie. He twists, his hand landing flat on the center of my back to push me further into the room. "Bex, you remember Sam and Mike from school, right?"

I nod, offering them a smile. "Sure, how are you guys?"

"Good. Jess and I got married a couple years ago and just had a set of twin boys." This comes from Mike, his face beaming in pride as he speaks.

"That's amazing! Everyone knew you and Jess would get hitched one day." I address Sam. "What about you? How have you been? Anything new and exciting happening with you?"

His gaze shifts to Max for an instant and then back to me, his large hand raking through his short auburn locks. His eyes dart toward the floor when he finally replies. "Yeah, ah, Stacy and I just got engaged this past summer. Wedding is going to be next fall."

"Oh." I clear my throat, my mouth suddenly parched as

the Sahara. Stacy and Sam had just broken up the week before I saw Max kissing her, so to hear him announce their engagement is a surprise. I force the corners of my mouth to lift. "I had no idea you were back together. That's great." I nod to reaffirm my statement. "I hope you'll be really happy."

He shrugs. "Yeah, I'm not sure what I was thinking back then, but there's definitely no one else for me but Stacy."

I wonder if he knows about Max and her, but before I can say anything else, I feel myself being propelled across the kitchen to a door leading to the rec room. Max's hand still on my back as he explains our sudden exit. "We're going to go talk in the rec room." The crew shout out different variations of thanks, good to see you, and come visit again as we leave.

"Maxwell, stop pushing me." I twist out of his hold to face him. "What was that about?" I cross my arms, glaring up at him.

He mimics my stance, glaring right back at me. "You know how those guys are. If you get them started, they would have never let you leave. You would have been on the firing line about where you've been and what you've been doing since you left for the next hour."

"Oh." My temper shifting from a boil to a low simmer. "I thought you were trying to keep me away from Sam."

"Why would I care about you talking to Sam?" He pushes, knowing why, but forcing me to say it out loud.

"Does he know what happened between you and Stacy?" There, it's out. The first question that popped into my head when Sam said they were back together.

Max lets out a heavy sigh, shaking his head as his eyes roll towards the heavens. "Bex, nothing ever happened between Stacy and I. Nothing that warrants any actual concern. I'd be happy to explain if you'd ever let me."

"Okay." My arms still crossed over my chest, my chin thrusting out. "Let's hear it. Let's finally here what *didn't* happen between you and my best friend."

His eyes widening as he takes a step back. "Really?"

"Yep. Really." He doesn't need to know that I came down here to have a civil conversation about this very subject with him. It seems that fate made some decision that it was time for us to finally tackle 'the kiss that ended it all'.

"Wow, okay." His fingers rub over the stubble lining his chin, his head cocking in disbelief. "Let's do this then."

He steps around me and walks to a table in the far corner of the room. He pulls a chair out and nods toward it, indicating I should sit. I do as requested; him pushing the chair in under me. Once I'm settled, he pulls out the chair besides me and does the same.

He clasps his hands in front of us on the table, then lifts his head to stare directly into my eyes. "Why now? I've tried to have this conversation with you a dozen times."

"I don't know, Max." I glance away from the intensity of his gaze. "Maybe because I'm not as angry as I was, or maybe because it's not as easy to hate you as I thought." My voice lowers, hovering just above a whisper. "Or maybe it's because I know now why you didn't talk to me at the funeral."

He frowns, his hands unclasping as one lifts to grasp the

back of his neck, still analyzing me intensely. "What did you think the reason was?"

"I thought it meant you had moved on. That there wasn't any reason to talk to me anymore." I pick at a hang-nail on my thumb when he remains silent. I'm not sure if he's angry or if it's because he's tired of having to defend himself, so I lift my eyes to his and spill out the next words like an apology. "I didn't know you found them, Max. I had no idea what you went through. I couldn't see through my pain to realize how much you were in as well. If only I hadn't let my pride get in the way, maybe we could have helped each other."

"You lost your parents, Bex." His cheeks expand as he blows out a breath. "I didn't have any expectations from you. You were grieving."

I slide a hand across the table and take his. "So were you."

His fingers tighten around mine, then slip out of my hold as he leans back in his chair. "This is getting a little heavy. You still want to talk about Stacy?"

I nod. "I do." I shift in my seat. "I think."

"Listen, it's not anywhere near as bad as you've imagined it in your mind." He starts.

"Oh, you think I imagined you kissing her?" I defend, my spine stiffening.

His lips pinch together as his fingers drum on the table. "Do you want to let me talk?"

"Fine." I blurt, crossing my arms again, huffing as I do.

"Jesus, you're stubborn woman." He chuckles, then continues. "Stacy and Sam had broken up the week before. I was spending a lot of time with them because of Sam and I attending the fire academy together, so I had a front-row seat to the meltdown of their relationship." He shakes his head, frowning at the memory. "They were fighting over the same stupid shit everyone does at that point in their relationship; Should we get married? Should we move in together? Does it mean I don't love me if we don't get a place? Am I settling or is there something better out there?"

"I guess we never got quite that far in our relationship." I muse out loud.

"You had been away at school the last four years. We would have gotten there eventually if-"

I cut him off, finishing the sentence for him. "If I hadn't caught you kissing Stacy."

"Bex, you didn't catch us," he uses his fingers to mimic air quotes around catch us, "because we weren't doing anything wrong."

I arch a brow and motion for him to continue. "Okay, fine. Whatever you say. Keep going."

He gives a slight shake of his head but continues. "When we were at the Christmas Eve Ball, I found Stacy sitting all alone in the back corner of the room. She had been crying and was missing Sam. I sat down and talked with her for a while, trying to comfort her, telling her to just give Sam some time. Told her what immature jerks we men were and that she just needed to be patient because I was sure he'd come around."

He stops then and glances back toward the kitchen, then at me. "Do you want some coffee? Sorry, I should have offered when you first came in."

"No, I don't want any coffee, Max!" I huff out. "I want you to finish the story."

"Alright, alright. Every time I try to be a nice guy, I get in trouble." He runs a hand down his face, but I think it's an attempt to hide the smile he's fighting to keep at bay.

I lean forward and give him a playful nudge. "Yeah, okay, Mr. Nice Guy, just get on with it already."

"I had gotten her to a point where she was feeling better enough to come back and join us. I headed us back to the table when she stopped to point up at some mistletoe that was hanging above us. She made a comment about how she wanted to rip it all down because every time she saw a couple kissing, it just made her miss Sam more, and made her feel even more alone. The poor girl was so sad, and I just wanted to make her feel a little better, so I bent down, gave her a kiss and I told her she wasn't alone. I told her that she had me and you, and a bunch of other people that loved her."

"And that's when I stepped in and pushed you two apart, slapping you pretty hard in the face if I recall." I face plant into my palm, shaking my head, afraid to look at him.

"Uh, yeah, you definitely left a mark." He chuffs. "I couldn't find you that night, and the next day was Christmas. When I could finally get to your house that afternoon, you'd already gone back to New York. Your mom informed me you left, and that you took the internship that publishing house had offered you."

I fold my arms on the table and hide my face there. How could I have been so wrong, so stupid, so blind to the fact that he wouldn't have hurt me like that? Actually, I knew why, but

I was ashamed to admit it, even to myself, until this very moment. Stacy was always the beautiful one, the adored one, captain of the cheer team, valedictorian of the class, dressed in the most recent trends. I had pretended none of that bothered me, because I had Maxwell Chastain. Best looking, most popular football captain, loved by the town, three years older, and yet, he wanted me, not her. Like everyone else. Until I saw them together that night. A fury ignited in me like none I had ever experienced before. And you know what it was? Mrs. Chastain was correct. It was my pride. My damn pride became more important than anything else. And to save face, I ran. Instead of letting him tell his side of things, only assuming the worst. How could I explain any of this to him and have it make sense? The truth was, I couldn't. Because what I did was foolish and selfish, and the biggest mistake of my life.

"Are you going to say anything?" His fingers brush through my hair, moving the strands to reveal my hidden face.

"Why?" I peer up at him.

His brow creases. "Why what?"

"Why did you bother?" I straighten, keeping my focus on him.

"Why did I bother with you?" He echoes my question, like maybe he's not sure why I would ask such a silly question.

"Yes." I nod. "I didn't deserve it." I shake my head once, correcting myself. "I *don't* deserve it. I didn't even have enough faith in you to give you the benefit of the doubt. I wouldn't let you explain. No matter how hard you tried. I sent at least a dozen letters back to you unopened. I wouldn't take your calls." I slam my fist down onto the table, but it only makes a soft thumping sound. "I punished you for something you didn't even do!"

"Because I loved you." He murmurs.

Loved. There it is. As in, I loved you once, but not anymore. And there is no one to blame but myself. I did this. I pushed him away and made sure I kept him there.

I do what I should have done five years ago. I apologize and I hope he'll forgive me. "I'm sorry, Max. I'm so sorry. I was wrong, and a fool, and I-"

"You're forgiven." He interrupts my plea, his hands reaching across the table to grasp onto mine. "Apology accepted."

"But-" Confusion swirls through my mind, my mouth agape as I stare back at him.

"It's enough, Bex." His grip softens, his fingers lacing through mine. "Enough time wasted, enough pain shared, enough love lost. No more, okay?"

"Okay." A surge of relief spreads through my body, warmth invading my heart, which, only moments ago, felt cold and hollow. How could I have ever pushed this man away? Before I can ponder the thought further, the alarm bell sounds throughout the station, followed by the dispatcher announcing a multi-vehicle 10-50 with confirmed injuries on Mountain Vista Road, one half mile past the Colonial House Restaurant.

Max untangles his fingers from mine and jumps up. "I have to go. It's a car accident."

"Of course!" I stand up too, waving him off. "Go! I'll talk to you later."

He strides off, then stops, turning back to me. "I still have things I want to say to you."

I just nod. Of course he does. He should. I knew forgiveness was never this easy. Before I can find any words, he twists back around and sprints toward the trucks.

"Be safe." I call out, not sure if he hears me or not, but hoping he does.

Chapter Five

I make my way back home, and to kill some time, take Hercules for another walk. We only make it about a quarter of a mile before I have to pick him up and carry him. I put a sweater on him before we left, but his little paws were freezing cold from the cement of the sidewalk. I bring us back to the house, light a fire, and then curl up on the couch with a book. It takes less than ten seconds for Hercules to jump up beside me and snuggle up in a tight ball against my waist. I open my book and lose myself in the highlands of Scotland, eventually drifting off to sleep.

"Hey sleepyhead, wake-up." A warm breath of air floats across my skin, a soft voice trying to coax me awake. I blink, my eyes popping wide when I realize someone is hovering over me, my hand moving over my fluttering heart when I register it's Max.

"Did you sneak in again?" I groan in frustration, looking

down at Hercules, my useless alarm system, then grumble. "This dog is fired as my bodyguard."

"I knocked." He's squatting next to me, his hair glistening and wet, I'm assuming from a recent shower. "But when you didn't answer, I let myself in." He reaches out to scratch the dog's head. "See? You might as well have gotten a cat."

I roll my eyes, then look out the window to see if I can gage what time it is. "How late is it?"

"Not very." He glances at the watch strapped on his wrist. "Just a little after two."

"It feels later." I yawn, lifting my arms over my head as I stretch, my cheeks bursting with heat when I sense his gaze roaming down my body. I jerk to a sitting position, but then find my legs inside his, not helping in my attempt to put some space between us.

His hands lift off his thighs to shift onto each of mine, his long fingers gripping around the width of my legs easily. I peek up through my lashes to find him staring at me with an intensity that has my mouth parting, my tongue darting out to sweep across my lower lip. My pulse races, my breath quickening, and I lean forward, closing my eyes when his palm falls against my cheek. His warm, full lips press against my forehead, my lids snapping open as his hold on me releases and I watch him rise to his full height. *What the hell? A forehead kiss?*

"Let's go ice skating." He suggests before I can utter a sound of protest over his friendly kiss.

"Ice skating?" I repeat, making sure I heard him correctly, getting up from the couch.

"Ice skating." He confirms. "The snow is starting tonight, and then the pond will be covered. Remember how much fun we used to have?" He snags my hand and pulls me toward the mudroom. "I know your skates still have to be in here somewhere."

"I don't remember having that much fun." I argue. "I remember you playing hockey with all the guys, and me twirling around trying to get your attention."

"That's the part I remember." He winks at me. "Those cute little skirts you would wear with the white tights. When you twirled around, I would get the best view of your ass."

"Max!" I admonish, my cheeks lifting against my will, as he finds my skates on the shelf and hands them to me. "Don't be crude."

"You think that's crude?" He chuckles. "I guess I won't tell you what else I was thinking." He smacks me lightly on the ass, then runs out of the mudroom. "You still got any of those skirts up in your room?"

"Even if I did, I'm not going to wear it now!" I chide as I follow him. "I believe I'll go throw on my thickest snow pants and heaviest coat." I stick my tongue out at him as I sprint up the stairs to change.

"Party pooper!" He calls out. "Meet me out back when you're ready!"

"Yep!" I shout back, skidding to a stop in front of my dresser. I pull open drawers until I find what I'm looking for and then change as fast as I can. I sprint back downstairs to the mudroom to pull on my cute, white fluffy pullover, and find the matching hat and mittens putting them on. I stuff my feet into my tan Ugg's, then yank the back door open.

"Ta-da!" I spin in a circle as I step outside, my skirt lifting from the motion. "Don't ever accuse me of being a party pooper!" I cock my head and flash a triumphant grin.

"Oh, you *think* you're the winner here, but I've clearly won the battle." His dimples appearing as he grins broadly. "And you, my little snow angel, are all the reward I need."

I know it's a minor victory, but I give it to him. I owe him that, and so much more after what I've put him through the last five years. I'm still a little in awe that he has forgiven me so easily. I'm not sure I would have been able to do the same if the shoe had been on the other foot. That he can still look at me, how he is right now, gives me so much hope.

I beam back at him as I dip into a small curtsey. "One snow angel at your service." I straighten, locking eyes with his, an undeniable attraction building between us as we stare at each other for a moment in silence.

"Come." He holds his hand out, curling his fingers around my mitten'd ones, and helps me down the stairs. He's got our old milk crates in his other hand, our skates secure inside. "Let's get on the ice before it gets too late."

We walk through my backyard, and then onto the short path through the woods until we reach the edge of the pond. I stop short, my breath taken away by the beauty before me. "I forgot how much I love this place."

"When's the last time you were here?" He releases my hand to take the skates out of the crate, then flips it over, patting the top of it.

"I don't remember." I murmur. "It's been years." I sit, and he kneels before me. He pulls off my boots, and then stretches one of my skates wide, slipping it smoothly onto my foot. I laugh out loud, and he stops tightening my laces to look up at me. "I feel like Cinderella right now." I try to suppress my glee by holding my hand over my mouth.

He gives a slight shake of his head, one side of his mouth quirking up. "Happy to be your Prince Charming for the day."

"Just the day?" I tease, fluttering my lashes at him.

"I guess we'll see what happens when the clock strikes midnight." He flashes me a coy smile, then returns his attention back to my laces. I sit in silence as he does the same with my other skate, not speaking until he stands and reaches out to me with both hands.

"Up you go." I grab onto him, and he yanks me up. "Let's see if you still got skills."

"Oh, I still got skills, don't you worry about that." I drop his hands, step onto the ice, and push off in one hard motion, sending myself gliding across the ice. I spin around and begin skating backwards, taunting him. "Better hurry up and get those skates on or you'll never catch me!" I spin in a circle, making sure he gets a clear shot of my ass, then zoom off across the pond, giggling with delight.

I slow down after a few minutes, letting myself glide in a zig-zag pattern across the ice, enjoying the crisp cool air on my cheeks, while the last hour of sunlight for the day shines down on us. I look up and can see clouds moving in from the west, and wonder how much longer it will be until the snow starts.

"Gotcha!" Strong hands latch around my waist, a shriek of surprise escaping my lungs, as Max holds me tight and spins me around to face him. "You'll never be able to outrun me, even if you do have wings!"

"Oh, yeah?" I wrench myself from his grip to spin around again and start racing to the other side of the pond. I know he's stronger and faster than me, but having him chase me is exhilarating.

He flies by me, snatching my hat off my head as he does, and waves it in the air. "Come and get it!"

I dart after him, pressing my skates into the ice, pushing as hard as I can to try to catch up to him, but he keeps pulling ahead. He spins, skating backwards, and starts taunting me, throwing the hat under his leg, over his head, and even tries putting it on. I'm flying, going so fast, getting so close, when suddenly his skate hits something sticking up out of the ice and he goes down, slamming flat on his back against the ice. My hat goes airborne as his hands claw into the ice in an attempt to slow his momentum, a grimace plastered across his face.

To make matters worse, I was so close to him, I'm having a hard time stopping, dragging my toe pick as deep as I can when it snags onto the same object, sending me flying. I spread my arms out in front of me, bracing for impact, landing directly on top of Max's torso, both of us grunting out loud. I drag my mittens on the ice, until we finally stop moving.

I shove myself up, trying to take as much weight as I can off his body in case he's hurt, straddling his waist, my eyes darting to his face. "Oh my God! Are you okay? Are you hurt?"

I try digging my skates into the ice so I can stand, but his hands latch around my waist to hold me in place. "Where do you think you're going?" He smirks up at me.

Relief surges through me when I realize he's okay. I swat him lightly before dropping my head onto his chest, a breath I didn't know I was holding escaping in a rush. "That scared the shit out of me."

"I'm fine." His arms wrap around my back, pulling me tighter to his chest, warms lips pressing against the top of my head.

I can feel his heart beating like the hooves of a hundred horses under my ear though, so I know he was more scared than he's letting on. I try to lighten the moment by cracking a joke. "Caught you." I follow it up with a short laugh.

"You sure did." He mumbles against my head.

"Should we get up?" I ask. "Your back must be freezing, and I want to make sure it's okay."

"One more minute." His hold staying firm. "It's been five years since I've been able to do this."

My heart cracks just a fraction, knowing the five years was because of my stubbornness. I nod, not sure how to respond, but agree in silence that I'll lie here as long as he wants me to. After more than a minute, he speaks, and what he says surprises the hell out of me. "I came to New York to see you once."

"What?" I sit up, because I need to see his face for this. "When?"

"I don't know." He plays with the edge of my skirt. "It

was about a year after you left. A week or so before Christmas."

"But," I frown down at him, "You didn't come see me?"

"I saw you." He sits up then, his teeth clenching.

"You're hurt." I state, immediately pushing my body off his. "Let me look at your back." I skate behind him, but before I can bend to look at him, he rises off the ice.

"I'm okay." He faces me. "Just a bit sore from the fall." His hand rubs absently against his lower back. "Come on, let's go back to the house."

"Okay." I snag my hat off the ground and pull it over my head, then grab his hand in mine. "but we're going slow this time."

"You got it, Cinderella." He looks over at me and smirks.

"I want to know what happened in New York." I shoot back instead, my curiosity definitely getting the best of me.

He nods. "I'll tell you. I'm not trying to keep it a secret from you." He looks up at the sky, snowflakes drifting in slow motion from the heavens and down around us. "Here comes the snow."

I reach my hand up to catch some flakes as we glide, most of them melting as soon as they land on my mitten. "It's so beautiful."

"Sure is." I glance over and realize he's looking at me, not noticing the snow at all. And even though it's below freezing, I feel my cheeks flush with heat and realize that Maxwell Chastain is still in love with me.

Chapter Six

We burst into the mudroom, shaking the snow off as we slam the door behind us. It's only been fifteen minutes since flakes started flying, but the ground is already blanketed in white. We were definitely in for one heck of a storm. Hercules comes bounding into the room barking, skidding to a halt when he sees us, his tail wagging wildly instead. We greet him and then peel off our layers and move into the kitchen with him at our heels. He stays for a moment and then trots back off to his spot on the couch.

"Off." I point to the thermal shirt Max is still wearing. His brows arch high as he crosses his arms. "I want to look at your back to make sure it's okay."

"I told you, I'm fine." He leans against the counter, a coy smile lifting the corners of his wind-chapped lips. *Not that I was looking at his red, puffier than usual, begging to be kissed lips.* "There are better ways to get me to take my shirt off."

"Don't flatter yourself." I roll my eyes dramatically in a

vain attempt to pretend it's not what I want more than anything. "You aren't that pretty, Max." *It's not like I noticed how defined his abs looked, even with a layer of cotton covering them.* "This is totally out of medical necessity."

"Uh-huh." He snorts, unfolding his arms to grasp the hem of his shirt to pull it over his head. "Whatever you say, Nurse Ratched."

My eyes trail up each inch of skin as it's exposed, drinking in the thin trail of dark hair leading to the ripples of his washboard stomach, up to a chest sprinkled with auburn curls over pecs of steel. *Holy shit. He did not look like this the last time I saw him with his shirt off.*

"Close your mouth before your tongue falls out." He rumbles, trying not to smile.

"What?" I snap my gaze up to his face.

"I think it was my back you wanted to check out?" He smirks.

"Shut up." I quip, lifting my finger to make a circular motion. "Turn around!" He does as I command, albeit while chuckling, and holy crap, his back is as nice as his front. I only notice for a second though because my attention is diverted to a large bruise turning purple on the center of his lower back. I step closer to press my hand flat against the bruise. His skin feels hot where my hand lands and he hisses, flinching when I apply pressure. "Max, this is a terrible bruise, and it's right on your spine."

"Am I cut or bleeding?" He inquires over his shoulder.

"No."

"Does it feel like any bones are cracked when you press down?"

I prod his spine with my fingertips but I don't know what the hell it's supposed to feel like and all it seems to do is cause him more pain. "I don't feel any sharp edges. What's it supposed to feel like?"

He twists suddenly, spinning around to face me, my hand now resting on his stomach instead of his back. I lay it as flat as I can over the bumps, lifting my chin to look at him. He glances down at my hand, then back to my face, the laugh lines around his eyes no longer on display. "I'm fine. Nothing I haven't already had playing hockey and fighting fires."

"But-"

His finger lands over my lips, stopping my protest. "The only thing I notice right now, is how good your touch feels on my skin." My mouth parts slightly, and I think he believes I'm going to talk because he shakes his head. But I don't, because my heart is stuck somewhere in my throat making it hard for me to breathe, let alone utter a single word. His finger trails softly over the length of my bottom lip, his eyes tracking the movement, my other hand finding its way onto his chest.

"I've wanted to kiss you since the second I saw you in the store five days ago." He confesses, his finger still on my mouth. "I wanted to know if you still tasted the same. If you still pant when my tongue thrusts against yours. If you-"

"Yes!" I throw my hands around his neck, arching up to slam my lips against his. His arms engulf me, tugging me flush to his body, our kissing frantic as our mouths reunite again after so long. "Yes." I exclaim between breaths, one hand grasping the hair at the nape of his neck as I try to get even closer.

"God, I've missed you so much." He breaks away long enough to groan out, nipping his way down my neck, his hand clawing at the back of my shirt to raise it, his palm finally landing on my bare back.

I wrap one leg around his, angling my body to relieve the ache between my legs, his hands gripping my waist, my ass landing on the counter a second later. We pull apart long enough for me to rip my shirt over my head, our lips grinding together as soon as it's off. Max's fingers tangle in my hair and yank my head back, his tongue leaving my mouth to weave a wet trail down my neck to the top of my breast.

I'm panting, our hips grinding into each other, lost in the complete ecstasy of his mouth when I hear a shout from the living room. We both freeze and then jump apart when we hear Hercules start to bark.

"Shit!" Max pulls me off the counter and sets me on the floor, reaching down to grab my shirt. "It's my God damn mother!"

I struggle to get the shirt right side out and over my head before she walks in the room, but see her entering as my head pops through the top, my hair still stuck under the collar. My cheeks are on fire as I gush out the first thing that pops into my head. "This isn't what it looks like!"

"Oh, no?" She laughs out loud, pointing a finger at us both. "I'd say it looks like the two of you have kissed and made up. Literally." She laughs again, then gives Max a stern look. "Put a shirt on for goodness' sake, and button your damn pants."

My head swings in his direction. *When did that happen?* I'm sure my face is beet red and all I want to do is crawl under the table I'm so mortified. He turns his back to his mother to grab his shirt, mumbling under his breath. "Cock blocked by my own damn mother."

"I heard that." She states, walking closer, setting a bag onto the counter, her focus shifting to Max's back. "What on earth happened?"

He wrenches his shirt over his head, covering his body, turning back to her. "Nothing. I'm fine. Just fell on the ice."

"Don't 'fine' me." She barks. "Turn around and let me look."

"Mom, Bex already checked it. It's okay, I promise."

She snorts, not taking no for an answer as she lifts the back of his shirt. "Yeah, I can see how well that exam was going."

My eyes pop wide, and the mortification I was just getting over is back in full force.

"Jesus Christ, Mom. I'm thirty years old. I'm not a little boy anymore." He pulls away from her probing fingers and walks around to the other side of the counter.

"You're always going to be my little boy." She chuffs. "Get used to it." She places a hand on her hip, then looks between the two of us, a smile finally appearing. "I saw you two skating on the pond and thought you might be hungry. I brought over some beef stew I made." She nods toward the bag. "There are some fresh rolls in there as well."

"Oh." I say, still feeling like a girl caught with her skirt up in the back seat of a car after prom. "That was nice of you."

"Uh-huh." She gives us both that look only a mother can deliver. "Well, I'm not going to stay. Snow's getting bad. Just walked over to drop that off."

"Thanks, Mom." He goes to her and hugs her. "Want me to walk you back?"

"I assumed you were staying?" Her brow arches high.

"Um, yeah." He glances over at me and I nod, showing I want him to stay. "But I can still walk you back."

She pats him on the arm condescendingly. "I'm a big girl. I think I can make it a couple thousand feet down the road."

"I know that." He bites back. "But it's snowing pretty hard out there. Just text me when you get home so I know you made it safely."

"I will, but I texted before I came over and you can see what a fat load of good that did me." She states dryly, then breaks into a wide grin. "But I can also see that you were pretty busy."

"Mom." He rakes a hand through his hair. "Enough, already."

"Okay, okay." Still smiling, she turns to head out of the kitchen. "You two kids be good now! Don't do anything I wouldn't do!"

An hour later, after devouring the stew and bread Denise brought for us, we head into the living room and get comfortable on the couch, Hercules jumping up between us. We had both changed into some comfy clothes before eating; me into my pj's and Max into an old pair of Jonny's sweats and a t-shirt.

"You want me to start a fire?"

"That would be amazing."

I watch as Max rolls up an old newspaper and then places kindling over it, finally lighting a match, igniting the paper until it flames to life. Once it's going strong, he places a few logs on top and then comes back to sit next to me.

"So, will you tell me about New York?"

"Sure." He adjusts himself on the couch, moving so he's facing me. "Like I said earlier, it was before Christmas. I think about a week before. I was pissed because I had gotten another returned letter in the mail from you."

He scoffs at the memory but continues. "I didn't even stop to think. I just knew I had enough of your silence. I got in my truck and drove six straight hours until I somehow found myself parked in front of your address." His fingers stroke the dog blindly as he peers across at me. "The problem was, once I actually got to your place, I wasn't really sure what I wanted to say." He chuckles. "You think I would have figured that out on the way, but nope. If I'm honest, I was scared shitless to see you again."

"Was I not home?" I ask, still trying to understand why I never saw him.

"Strangely enough, as I was sitting there trying to figure out my next move, I saw you. You were strolling down the sidewalk, your nose buried in your phone, never looking up when you entered your building."

He stands abruptly, my body bouncing slightly on the cushion of the couch. I open my mouth to speak, but then close it when he goes over to the fireplace and throws another log on. He turns, crossing his ankles, then his arms, and leans against the wall. "I finally found my balls and climbed out of the truck when you came out of the building, bundled up in workout clothes. I thought maybe you were going for a run, or a walk, so I waited until you were a ways down the street and then I followed you."

"Stalker." I joke, tossing a smile his way.

He chuckles in return. "Yeah, I guess I kind of was in that moment."

"Where'd I go?" I ask, not remembering at all what day he might be referring to. This was years ago, so it could have been anywhere.

"Central Park." He pauses a second, his eyes closing briefly, his face contorting as if in pain. "You went to an ice rink just off the edge of the park. You met some guy there. You hugged him, helped each other with your skates, and then went out onto the ice holding hands."

My brows shoot up as I remember exactly what and who he is talking about, but before I can tell him, he keeps going.

"I didn't need to see anymore." He looks down at his feet, his tone full of defeat as he recalls the memory. "The minute I saw you take his hand, it was like someone stuck a damn knife in my chest. I left. You had obviously moved on, and it was pretty clear why you returned all my letters."

"You may be a bigger dumbass than me." I exclaim, his head whipping up, eyes locking with my crinkled ones as I let out a small laugh.

"How's that exactly?" He unfolds his limbs, pushes off the wall and moves to sit beside me again.

"That wasn't a boyfriend." I give him a playful shove. "I wish you would have come over." I shrug, understanding why he didn't. We both let our pride impede things. "When I first moved to New York, I was so lonely. And I was sad. I missed you, I missed my family, I missed running into people I knew when I turned a corner or went in a store. During the day, I would lose myself in the books I was editing, but when I would leave the office at night, I just went home to an empty space. Most of the friends I had gone to NYU with had moved somewhere else, or were busy getting on with their lives."

"Yeah, I understand that. I felt like a hollow shell for more than a year after you left."

I frown, wishing I could go back in time to change that one stupid moment. Everything might be different now. "I'm so sorry, Max."

"No, I'm not trying to make you feel bad." He slips his hand over one of mine, weaving his fingers through mine.

"I know. But I do." My eyes drift to the flames dancing in the fireplace. "So much wasted time."

He squeezes his hold for a second, but doesn't let go. "Finish your story."

"So, anyway, I saw an article in one of the New York

magazines about a place that supported injured veterans, that was staffed by volunteers and financed by a man named Ben Sapphire."

"Like, from the Sapphire Resorts?" His brow furrows.

"Exactly." I nod. "Although, I didn't know that. I just thought if I could volunteer, maybe it would fill some of the void I was feeling."

"Did it help?"

"It really did." The dog yawns between us, stretches, and then jumps off the couch, trotting over to his bed near the fireplace. "Sometimes they had me work the front desk, other times I arranged their library for them, and the time you saw me, I was helping a marine who had lost part of his leg over in Afghanistan. He grew up in Northern Maine playing hockey, and he said the one thing he missed more than anything was skating. Ben worked with him for weeks to build up his strength until he finally felt ready to go strap on some skates. It was a huge deal. To make someone feel whole again just by holding their hand while they tried to do something they once loved. It was amazing."

"You're amazing." His gaze is intense as he stares at me, his palm heating the skin on the back of my hand.

I shake my head, lowering my eyes. "No, I'm not. Not even a little bit. What those soldiers sacrificed, that was amazing, and brave, and selfless. What I did doesn't even compare." I peer up at him. "What you do, that's amazing. You run into burning buildings. You tried to pull a thousand pound animal off an object to save people you love." I blink several times, but a tear still manages to leak and then trail down my cheek.

"No, no, no." His grip leaves mine, his fingers brushing away the moisture on my face. "Please don't go there. We've had enough blame and guilt and sadness already. It's time for us to leave the past behind and see what's ahead for us."

I bite my lower lip, wanting that more than anything, but not sure what we do to get there. He makes it easy for me when he grips me around the waist to hoist me over his lap in a straddling position.

"Let's start with this." And then he leans forward, pressing his lips softly against mine, his hands reaching around my back to pull my tight. I weave my arms around his neck and lose myself in everything that is him.

Chapter Seven

I wake the next morning, our legs tangled together in my bed. Max is still asleep, his beautiful face relaxed, and I can't help but wonder if Christmas morning has come early. I don't think I could get a better gift than Maxwell Chastain naked. I lift the covers to admire his extremely fit body, gasping when his voice rumbles above me. "See something you like?"

"I, uh, was looking for my, um, my shirt." I stutter like a dummy, afraid to lower the blanket, because I know my flaming cheeks will give me away.

"Sure you were." His chest vibrating with a deep chuckle. "You can look all you like. I don't mind."

"That's not what I was doing." I lie, yanking the covers over my face as I fling myself on my back.

Quick as lightning, the blankets tear from my grip, Max suddenly hovering over me. "I think we should stay here all day." He brushes his nose against mine and begins fluttering his perfect, puffy lips over every inch of my face.

"Shouldn't you go help your dad with snow removal?" I let out a soft moan as he sucks my earlobe between his teeth, his tongue darting out after licking the tender flesh. I arch my body up into his, my legs spreading as his hips sink into mine.

"He's a big boy. I sure he can manage without me for an hour." His breath hot against the moisture on my ear, before he moves his mouth lower to wrap it around my peaked nipple.

My fingers lace through his hair, digging into his scalp when he flicks the hard tip of my breast, then pulls it between his lips. "Okay, if you're sure." I pant out, cause, hey, who am I to argue with a grown man?

Almost two hours later, we drag ourselves from the bedroom and down to the kitchen. If it wasn't for Hercules, we might not have actually left. After several stern yips from him, he made it clear he needed to go out and needed to eat. We were pretty hungry too. After eating breakfast, okay, it's probably more accurate to call it lunch, we get dressed to head outside and see what we need to do about all the snow.

"Holy shit!" I shout in glee when I see the white, fluffy splendor. "We must have over a foot!"

"I'd say at least eighteen inches, maybe twenty."

"You think?" I jump off the porch steps into the deep powder, the accumulation reaching above my knee. "Whoa! You're right!" New York doesn't get snow like this, and I haven't come home for Christmas since, that Christmas, and it just feels magical. I trounce through the thick, settled flakes until I'm in the middle of the lawn, then turn and let myself fall back. I land with a whoosh and begin flapping my arms and legs. "Come make angels with me, Max!" I call out with glee.

A second later he flops down a few feet away, snorting, his arms and legs flying as he mimics my movements. "We haven't done this since we were kids."

"It's still so much fun!" I giggle as I try to lift myself up without ruining my creation.

"So much fun." He concurs, standing up next to me. "But, we probably should get your driveway and sidewalk taken care of."

I puff my bottom lip out in a fake pout which results in him grabbing it between his teeth before smothering my mouth in a heated kiss. Not the reaction I was expecting, but I sure wasn't going to complain. When he steps away, both of our breaths leave us in small puffy clouds. He flashes me a swoon worthy smile. "If we hurry, we might actually have time to take a nap before Jonny gets here later."

My brows shoot up at his suggestion, my smile appearing. "Okay, you just convinced me. Let's get this done!"

Six hours later, with the snow cleared and one nap achieved, I pull a lasagna out of the oven. I'm excited to see Jonny, Natalie and the kids. It's been over six months and I hope the kids still remember me. Chris is five and probably will, but Sara is only three, so I can't be sure. Max went home to take a shower, but was going to come back to have dinner with all of us.

I hear the crunching of snow in the driveway as headlights sweep across the windows in the front of the house, and I dart to the door to see if it's them. Hercules jumps from the couch, barking, even though I don't think he knows at what. I scoop him up and then tug the door open, waiting on the porch for everyone to unload from the van.

Natalie is out first, waving at me, a smile plastered on her face. "Hey Becca! Let me just get Sara out of her seat."

Jonny pops up on the other side of the van. "Hey, Sis!" He points at the house. "Lights look fantastic!" He flashes me a quick grin, then disappears as he bends to help Chris out.

I'm shifting from foot to foot, some of it impatience, some of it to try to keep warm, squealing in delight as they all finally climb up onto the porch. "I missed you guys so much!"

Sara tucks her head into her mom's shoulder, hiding her face, but Chris wraps his little arms around my thighs in a hug. "Hi Auntie Becca."

"Chris, you got so big!" I kneel in front of him, his interest immediately shifting from me to Hercules.

"Can I play with him?" His eyes light up, his hand darting out to pat the dog's back.

"Sure, let's just get inside." I press a quick kiss to the top of his head and then stand back up, my brother's arms folding me into him.

"It's been too long, Becca." He whispers into my ear. "You doing okay?"

We pull apart, my cheeks rising as I nod. "I'm good. Really good." I turn toward Nat and lean forward, pressing a kiss to her cheek. "Still beautiful, I see."

"Still a liar, I see." She retorts, laughing.

"Please!" I admonish. "You're gorgeous." I point to the kids. "I mean, these two definitely didn't get their looks from that one." I swing my gaze to my brother, winking.

"Yeah, yeah." He groans. "Always the comedian."

"Let's get inside where it's warm." I open the door and we all shuffle inside. Jackets and boots come off and as soon as I set Hercules on the floor, Chris lunges for him.

The dog sprints, Chris chases, and Nat moans. "Sorry."

"Please, no worries." I wave away her concern. "Believe me, that dog can hold his own for a little thing."

"The tree looks stunning!" Nat gushes, Jonny nodding in agreement. "Did you do that all by yourself?"

"I had a little help." I offer, but give them nothing more.

"I'm going to go out and grab our bags." Jonny announces, then leaves.

Nat and I move into the kitchen, Sara still sticking to her like glue. "So, tell me Becca, are you okay?" She stops, pries Sara from her neck, and sets her on a stool at the breakfast bar. "And don't give me that look. You know we were all worried about you being here alone."

"You want wine?" I snag a bottle out of the rack on the counter, holding it up.

"Hell, yes." She nods emphatically. "The biggest glass you have."

I giggle, complying as I find the largest wine goblet I can, and fill it up. "The first day was hard. Going into Mom and Dad's room. Not seeing all their stuff in there anymore."

"I know." She takes a gulp of the red liquid. "The first few times Jonny and I spent the night in there felt weird. Like we were doing something wrong."

"I just miss them. But actually, being here made me feel a little closer to them." I pour myself a glass and take a sip. "There's so much I need to catch you up on." I give her a nervous smile. "Things have gotten pretty interesting around here."

"Oh, yeah?" She cocks her head, putting a juice cup and a bowl of crackers in front of Sara. "Do tell."

Before I can share, Jonny strolls in, Max only one step behind. Nat's eyes fly from Max to me, her mouth falling open, forming a small O shape as her brows arch high.

"Look who I found wandering around outside." Jonny stops beside Nat, dropping an arm around her shoulder, cocking his head toward Max. Max strides past everyone else, halting when he gets to me, bends, and then captures my lips in a kiss. When he pulls away, both Jonny and Nat are staring wide-eyed.

"You two got some explaining to do!" Jonny proclaims, his face lighting up as he continues. "But God damn, it sure is good to see that you two have worked things out!"

Nat and I set the table for dinner, and after, while the

men clean up, we give the kids a bath and put them to bed. Over the summer, Nat and Jonny packed up all my parents' things and stored them in the attic. Someday, when I was ready, I would go through it all, but I wasn't there yet. They redecorated the room over and stayed there in that room now when they came. Jonny's old room got converted for the kids.

We hadn't decided what to do with the house long term. Jonny started his own law firm only three years ago, and it was just starting to prosper, so he and Nat didn't want to move here permanently. They loved coming up in the summer with the kids, and of course, for Christmas. I suppose everyone assumed that one day I would move back to the Valley and start a family here. My job was transferrable, and I was at a point where I could work from anywhere, but until this week, I hadn't pictured myself leaving New York.

Max and I had spent one night together, and approximately three days actually getting along. I had no idea what the future held for us. I knew though, without a doubt, that I was still in love with him. It was so strange. We hadn't spoken for almost five years. During those five years, of course I thought of him. If I'm honest, every single guy I dated, I measured up to him, and there was always that something that wasn't just right. Every attempt I made at a relationship failed. Being back here, being with him, it seemed as if the last five years never happened. It didn't seem real we had actually been apart that long. Time is a funny thing, I suppose, and the heart, even more so.

When Nat and I get back downstairs, we find the guys in

the living room, the fire going, and a fresh bottle of wine waiting for us.

"My hero!" Nat sings, pouring herself a hefty glass, then plopping a kiss against Jonny's lips as she sits next to him.

"I'm actually going to go make myself a cup of coffee." I yawn, reinforcing my choice. "Anyone else?" They all decline and I head to the kitchen. A few minutes into the pot brewing, I hear footsteps and turn, my lips curving into a smile. "Hey you." I reach my arms out, sliding them around Max's waist when he reaches me.

"You okay?" He holds me close. "You seem quiet."

"I'm good." I yawn again. "Just a little tired. Someone kept me up half the night, and I got way more exercise than I'm used to in the last twenty-four hours."

"You want me to go home tonight?" I pull away so I can look up at him as he continues. "I don't want to make it uncomfortable for you."

"Do you want to go?" My brows creasing.

"No. I want to stay. I'd never spend another night without you again if it was up to me." He admits, then begins back tracking when my eyes go wide. "Not that I'm trying to rush anything. I'll do whatever you want me to do."

"I want you to stay." I state softly, choosing not to address anything else he just blurted out.

"You know, right?" He looks down at me, his green irises softening, his palm cupping my face as he leans closer.

"Know what?" I whisper, my pulse racing, my chest rising and falling rapidly.

"I'm in love with you, Bex." He waits a second and when

I just stare back at him, he keeps going. "I don't know if I ever stopped. But you have to know. I love you."

I blink, my head shifting back and forth slowly. "Can this happen? Is this too fast?"

"Too fast?" His hand moves from my cheek to the back of my head as he yanks me flush to him. "It's been sixteen years, Bex. I think I knew I loved you when I was fifteen and you were twelve. Robbie Jarvis pushed you off the swing at the park, and I saw red. I wanted to pound him to a pulp. And it wasn't because you were my best friend's little sister. Even back then, I knew you were meant to be my girl." He shakes his head. "No, it's definitely not too fast."

"I can't believe I'm saying this already, but Max, I love you too." I don't get to say anything after that because he smashes his mouth to mine, sealing both of our admissions with a kiss that makes my head spin. I'm in love with Maxwell Chastian. Holy shit. Now what?

<h1>Chapter Eight</h1>

The next two days go by in a blur of Christmas shopping, present wrapping, visiting friends, dinner at the Chastain's, and some of the best sex I'd ever had. I was so grateful that my bedroom was on the far side of the house. Max and I had yet to figure out what was going to happen next for us, but I wasn't scheduled to head back to New York until after the new year, so I knew we had time to figure it out.

The hardest part of the last two days was tucking my tail between my legs to visit Stacy so I could offer her an apology. She was still as beautiful as ever, but she was also full of grace and accepted my apologies without making me feel worse than I already did. The fact of the matter was that we weren't in high school anymore. Even when we were, she was never competitive with me. That was me and my insecurities, and again, my pride, that severed a friendship we'd had our entire lives. I truly hoped we might get back to a place even better than when we were teenagers and knew only time would tell.

Coincidentally, tonight was the annual Green Mountain Valley Christmas Ball. The very same event in which I royally screwed up. I didn't want to go. The event felt like a talisman to the demise of my relationship with Max. Going again seemed like tempting fate, and I was happy again, after so long. Max, Jonny, and Nat insisted we go though, promising a night of friends, dancing, booze and laughter. I finally relented and now found myself two towns over trying to find a last-minute dress to wear.

"What about this one?" Nat held up a red backless number that might fit me if I slathered myself in Vaseline.

"Seriously?" I challenge. "Maybe in my next life."

"I think you would look hot in this." She holds the dress up to my body.

I cringe. "Absolutely not." I hold up a black dress, with a long silk skirt with a lace top. "What about this?"

"I mean, it's gorgeous, but black?" She shrugs, sneering. "It lacks the Christmas spirit."

"Ugh!" I grumble. "We've been at this for hours. Maybe I should just wear my old green dress in the closet at home?"

"Over my dead body." She warns. "You're getting something new."

I plop down on a round cushion that seemed to be placed strategically around the shop and watch as she slides one hanger into another on a rack. She stops, her face lighting up, and then pulls a dress out, holding it up for me. "This is the one."

I stare at it, and while I hate to admit it, I think she may have found a winner. It's white, which is the last color I would have picked out. But it has beaded crystals sewn in a way that shimmer and sway when the dress moves. The skirt looks to be mid length and a soft, billowy material, the top scooping into a low V, with short sleeves that match the material of the skirt. "It's stunning." I mutter, rising to walk over so I can get a closer look.

"It's your size too!" Nat exclaims. "It's a sign!"

"Let's go try it on!" I agree, just as excited.

She thrusts the hanger into my hand, pointing to the dressing room. "Go. Get started. I have to find the perfect shoes now."

Three hours later, I step slowly down the staircase, Max's expression confirming every thought Nat had about the dress. It was perfect. I've curled my normally straight auburn locks into long, loose waves, and Nat applied my makeup. When I reach the bottom, Max takes my hand, the dimples on his face deeper than usual by the enormous smile he gives me. "You look like an angel."

"It reminded me of my skating outfit." I say, a little shyly.

"Babe, this is a thousand times better." He cocks his head in appreciation. "You're absolutely breathtaking."

"Thank you, Max." I scan him from head to toe, appreciating how amazing he looks in his dark suit, the crisp white shirt he's wearing a perfect match to my dress. "You don't clean up so bad yourself. I love seeing you in your jeans and work boots, but I'm kind of digging this business look on you."

"Okay, if you two are just about done, can we get going

now?" Jonny bemoans from a few feet away. "I'm about to puke from the absolute saccharin overload going on."

"Don't be a dick." Max turns and jabs him in the upper arm. "You're just jealous cause I've always been better looking than you."

"Yeah." Jonny snorts. "You figured me out."

We all get our coats on and then load into my car, Max driving. Bill and Denise offered to take the kids for the night over at their house, so Nat and Jonny are more excited than a couple of kids in a candy store to have an entire night to themselves. It takes about fifteen minutes to get to the high school. It takes a few more minutes to find a spot, but we finally do, and park. In a town as small as Green Mountain Valley, there aren't a lot of options to hold an event that will hold more than a hundred people. You either get the high school gym, or you get the warehouse at the Army Reserve station one town over. The gym was a little nicer, believe it or not, and it's where the Ball has been for as long as I could remember.

We get inside, check our coats, and instantly lose Nat and Jonny as they race to the bar. I guess if I had two toddlers under the age of five, I'd want a few drinks too. Max weaves his fingers through mine, never letting go as we move through the crowd. We stop at least twenty times to reunite with old friends, surprise the first emotion express when they see us together. As I said earlier, in a town this small, everyone that lived here five years ago, absolutely knew me and Max's history.

When we finally make it across the room, we grab a couple drinks from the bar, and sit at a table on the far end of the dance floor. He points out people I haven't seen in ages, and catches me up on all the history. Nat and Jonny spot us and cruise in our direction, grabbing us all another round at the bar, then join us.

"Hey, did you see that asshole, Tony Riggs?" Jonny asks, looking over me at Max.

"Oh yeah, saw him a little while ago trying to hit on Debbie McAllistair."

"God, I hate that little prick." Jonny grumbles.

"For Christ's sake." Nat hops up from her seat to rearrange herself in Jonny's lap. "I dated him for two weeks. My sophomore year. You need to get over it."

"Prick knew I liked you, though. And only went after you because he knew I did." His eyes turn to slits as he focuses on Tony across the gym. "I should have kicked his ass back then."

"Come on, tough guy." She grabs his hand, laughing. "Let's go dance. I'll let you hang all over me so he can see I'm still yours." He follows her, smacking her ass before yanking her up against his body, sneering at Tony, and we both shake our heads.

"Boys will always be boys." I mutter, chuckling, then turn to him. "He's not going to start a fight with him, right?"

"Nah. He's just pissing on his territory. He'll be fine."

"So now he's a dog?"

"Babe, we've all got a little hound dog in us." He grins over at me. "It's just our nature. Part of our country boy charm."

"Oh, good lord." I feign my disapproval, but in truth, I wouldn't change a single thing about Max.

He stands from his seat, turns to me and extends his hand. "Let's go dance."

We spend the next half hour on the dance floor, spinning, waltzing, and laughing until we're out of breath and our feet need a break. Nat and Jonny come with us to grab some waters and a breath of fresh air. When we come back inside, the DJ is on a break, so the dance floor is empty. "Let's go sit over there." Max points to a table that appears to be available.

When we sit down, I look over and notice Stacy and Sam, under a spring of mistletoe, their lips locked together. I smile, relieved that she seems to be happy, and really wish her the best. It's funny how things turn out. My life is right where I thought it would be, even with the five-year gap. I guess when things are meant to be, they will be. I turn, looking at Max. "You want to go?"

His brows shoot up. "You not having a good time?"

"I've had a great time." I cover his hand with mine. "I've had enough though, and really just want to be with you."

He stands. "Let's go then." He looks down at Jonny and Nat. "You guys going to stay, or you want to come back with us?"

"Nah." Johnny waves his hand. "We'll get a ride from someone. We're going to stay."

"Call my cell if you can't find a ride." Max holds his phone up. "I'll come back and get you."

"We'll be fine. Thanks, though." We say our goodbyes, grab our coats, and head home. When we step inside the house, it's blissfully quiet. Hercules doesn't even rise from his bed, just lifts his head, looks at us, then goes back to sleep.

"I forgot how peaceful the house is when there aren't kids running around." I muse. We hang up our jackets and go into the living room. I flick the switch for the tree, the thousand white lights I strung on it casting a soft, twinkling glow around the room. Max moves to turn a lamp on, but I stop him. "Let's just leave the tree on. It's so pretty."

"Sure." He saunters back to me, a devilish gleam in his eye. "You wanna dance?"

"There's no music." I note, tilting my head, pretending to listen.

He pulls his phone out of his pocket, presses a few buttons, and a second later a soft melody plays. He places the phone on the coffee table and then holds his hand out. I place mine in his, and he tugs, lifting his arm to twirl me around, and then pulls me into his body. I drape my hands over his shoulders, sighing, knowing that I will never tire of being in his arms.

"Did you have fun tonight?" He asks, his breath warm against my head as we sway.

"I did. It was nice to see so many of our old friends." I snuggle closer to him.

"I know we have so much to figure out." His arms tighten around me. "Where we're going to live; my house, your house, your place in New York. Or maybe a new place completely. And our jobs." He stops moving, and then slides down my body until he's on one knee in front of me, my hand flying up to my mouth. "But baby, I love you. And I don't want to spend any more time without you. We've already lost five years. I'll go where ever you want, just as long as we can do it as husband and wife."

He reaches his hand into the inside pocket of his suit coat, a ring between his fingers when it appears again. "Please do me the honor of marrying me. Let's spend the rest of our lives together. I promise, I'll never break your heart and will do everything in my power to make sure every single day of our life is filled with nothing but happiness."

I stare at his face, and then at the ring, my heart stuttering to a halt when I focus on it. Tears spring from my eyes, dripping from my lashes when I blink, as I swing my gaze back to him. "Is that my mom's ring?"

He nods, the corners of his eyes filling. "I know I could have bought you a ring. Hell, I had one in my pocket five years ago. But Jonny suggested I give this one to you, and when he offered, I knew it was perfect. A way for your mom to always be with us."

I can barely see through the tears streaming down my face as I bounce my head up and down, agreeing to every word he's saying. "I love you so much, Max." I proclaim, my entire being filled with joy.

"Is that a yes?" He laughs nervously, brushing away the tears that have managed to escape.

"Yes!" I surge forward, throwing my arms around him, almost knocking him back. "A thousand times, yes!"

Epilogue

One Year Later

We stayed in Green Mountain and moved into my parent's house. We rent his house out seasonally, making sure we leave it open for any visits Bill and Denise make. My publishing house was great about letting me transfer my position, allowing me to work remotely, as long as I agreed to come to New York once a quarter.

We got married in June, right out back next to the pond. I wore my mother's wedding dress, and now her wedding ring set on my left hand. I think of her every time I look at it. I still miss her, and my dad. Especially now that I'm going to be a mom, but I know with all my heart that they are both looking down on me and would be so happy.

"Do you think we should get the blackberry and the raspberry jam for the cookies, or just the blackberry?" I pick up both jars, then put them both back, unable to decide.

"Bex, whatever you choose will be delicious." He pecks me on the cheek. "You know I love your cookies, no matter what flavor they are."

"Okay, I'll get both." I answer, putting a jar of each in the basket he's holding for me. "I think we need more flour too, so let's grab that while we're here."

"You got it, little momma." He smiles down at me, placing a hand over the small bulge that used to be my waistline. "Whatever you and this little one desire."

"Well, if she gets her way, it would be another pint of mint chocolate-chip ice cream." I giggle, rubbing my belly.

"Wait, did you say she?" He stops short in the aisle, turning to me. "I thought you said you didn't ask the doctor?"

"Well, he might have written it on a piece of paper and put it in a sealed envelope." I look up sheepishly. "And I might have held it up to the light last night when I couldn't stand not knowing anymore."

"Oh my God!" He chides. "You are a little sneak!"

"I couldn't help myself!" I defend. "Blame it on the hormones."

He drops to his knees, the basket landing on the floor, his hands spanning over the width of my belly. "We're having a daughter." He beams up at me. "A little girl." He places a soft kiss to the bump and speaks to her. "I can't wait to meet you little one."

The End

Afterword

Thank you so much for reading my first holiday romance. If you've already read me, I hope you caught the little nugget I left for you. If you're a new reader, thanks so much for taking a chance on me. No matter which you are, I hope you enjoyed this little escape.

xoxo

Michelle

Reviews mean so much to an author, so if you'd like to leave a sentence or two about the book, it is truly appreciated.
Review link:
https://bit.ly/JustOneXmas

You can find information about all my other work, including purchase links, on my website:
https://www.authormichellewindsor.com

If you liked this sweet story, you will probably enjoy my book called Catching Chase. It's another second chance romance, but it definitely has a few more steamy scenes as well. Just keep flipping the pages for a special preview. You can also check it out here:

https://bit.ly/catchingchase

As always, I'd like to thank my husband and children for all their encouragement and support on the nights I'm locked away in my office writing, editing, and doing book research. You've put up with a heck of a lot of takeout over the years without a single complaint. Love you guys so much.

A huge thank you to Lydia Michaels. For so many things that I'm sitting here struggling with where to start. Mostly of course, for your friendship. For making me laugh on days I want to curl up and die. For pushing me to sit back down and write, but also understanding when I just couldn't. For letting me bounce ideas off of you, and not being afraid to tell me when they suck. For helping with the cover. And most importantly, for diving into the deep end with our fucking fins up!!!!

To my tribe of book friends, who are always there when I need them, who share my books, my promos, and so much more without me even having to ask. Haylee, April, Cin, Cara, Nat/Ninja, Kendra, Leaona, Gina, Dusty, Cassidy, DD, Dakota, Pam, Carey, Sam, and I know I'm forgetting some, but please know, it's not intentional! It's just late as I'm writing this and my brain is exhausted! Thank you for your friendship and endless support.

An especially huge thank you to all the bloggers who let

me crash their pages, who share for me, who read and leave reviews for my books. I would not be here without you and your support! Thank you, thank you, thank you!

And one last thank you to my 'real-life' tribe; Jules, Mindy-Moo, Sir David, and Captain Bob. Jules, thanks for always, always being willing to be one of my very first read-throughs on my books and for your constant support. Mindy-Moo, you and Jules are my rocks, my diamonds, my friends-til-the-end bitches that make my life so much fuller by having you in it. Love you all so much and treasure every minute and martini we have together. David, Doug and Bob, thanks for always picking up our bar tabs...

XOXOXOXOXXOXOXOXOXOXOXOXOOXXOXOXOXO

Sneak Peek

I give a final wave as I step away from the podium at the front of the room, then make my way over to the steps leading off of the stage. I've just completed the last presentation required of me at my company's annual conference, and could not be more relieved. It's been a grueling four days of interaction as I tried to impress present and hopefully new clients with our products, and now I'm looking forward to some much needed downtime.

I weave my way out of the room as quickly as I can, only being stopped twice along the way to answer questions, heaving a sigh of relief when I reach the exit doors and push through them. I head in the direction of the elevators, my heels echoing across the tiled lobby floor when I hear my name being called.

"Megan?" I'm not sure if I'm the Megan in question, so I plant the toe of my shoe and spin in the direction of the voice. I freeze in place when my eyes connect with the person calling out my name.

"Megan! It is you." My heart rate accelerates, my pulse thundering in my ears so loud I can barely hear what he says next. "I almost didn't recognize you with your short hair." He's reached me now, and I still haven't uttered a word. I just stare at him in complete shock, a frown tarnishing his perfect lips as he points to himself. "It's Jasper. Please tell me you remember me."

I finally gather my senses and offer him a smile. "Of course I remember you Jasper." I lean forward, my fingers gripping his bicep in a loose hold as I brush an awkward kiss against his smooth cheek. I've never been this close to him when he's clean shaven. "I was just surprised to see you."

His hand sweeps against the blunt ends of my locks, just grazing the top of my shoulders. "Besides the hair, you haven't changed a bit." My hand releases his arm as I step back, my eyes fixating on his as my brain tries to catch up with my pulse. "What are you doing in Boston?"

"I'm here for a conference." I swing my gaze around the room, trying to find an exit strategy. "What about you?"

"I'm in town for the marathon. I'm meeting a couple of the guys for lunch." He shakes his head, sweeping a hand over the broad smile that's lighting up his face, like he's trying to either hide or contain his joy. "I can't believe it's really you. What's it been? Three years?"

"Almost four." I respond immediately, knowing exactly how long it's been. "Look, Jasper, I have to run, but it was lovely seeing you."

His brow creases at my obvious attempt to cut things short, not giving me the satisfaction as he tries to extend our reunion. "How long are you in town for? Do you want to have dinner tonight and catch up?" He glances for a moment at his feet, which are shifting back and forth in place, then continues. "I've wondered about you a lot over the years." He meets me in the eye, his tone becoming quiet. "There are things I'd like to say and explain."

My heart catches in my throat as I swallow down the feelings lodged there. I force a small smile to play on my lips. "Unfortunately, I'm heading up to my room now to gather my things to check out."

"Can I convince you to stay?" His palm is against my cheek before I can react, the memory of his skin against my own sending a jolt of pain to my very core.

I take a step back, his hand falling to his side as I shake my head. "I'm so sorry." I retreat another step. "I already have an obligation that can't be changed."

"Oh." His brow creases again as his lips curve downward. "Well, are you still in New York? I really would love to see you now that I've found you again."

"I really don't think that's a good idea." I walk away from him, trying to be as polite as I can without breaking into a run in an attempt to escape. "I'm sorry, but I really do have to go."

Unfortunately, he's not giving up that easily, and follows after me. "Megan, wait."

I pause mid-stride, closing my eyes in the hope that I can erase what's happening right now, opening them when I feel his hand wrap around mine to stop me. "Did I do something wrong?"

I turn to meet his eyes; his beautiful, unique eyes, and respond in a whisper. "No."

"Are you married?" He glances down to my hands, bare of any rings, then back to my gaze.

I can't help the short guff of laughter that tumbles from me at the irony of his question, releasing his hand. "No."

"Then what is it?" He pleads, wanting answers that I don't want to give. That I can't give. Not now. He's three years too late.

"Momma!" A voice I know better than any other calls excitedly from behind me, spiking the anxiety I was already feeling into near panic. Goosebumps prickle over every inch of my skin as I realize what's about to happen. Little arms wrap around my legs seconds later in a hug, his sweet voice muffled against my thigh as he says Momma again. I'm frozen like a deer caught in headlights, unable to look away from Jasper as his face displays several emotions in a row; surprise, shock, confusion, and then anger as they meet mine again. I lift my son to rest him on my hip, his eyes a mirror image of the man staring at us both, realization dawning across his features as his fingers splay over his gaping mouth.

In that same moment, my mother appears beside me, a little out of breath, but not so much that she can't chastise the boy in my arms. "Chase Montgomery Lewis! How many times do I have to tell you not to run away from Grandma like that?"

Jasper's wide eyes ricochet to mine. "His name is Chase?"

"What's going on?" My mother's head snaps back and forth as she tries to understand what's transpiring, a gasp bursting from her when she sees the resemblance between Jasper and Chase.

I nod, blinking rapidly to try and stop the tears that are threatening to spill from my water-rimmed eyes. *How is this happening right now? And why? Why now after all this time?*

Want to read more?

Click here: https://books2read.com/u/b6ZMdp

About the Author

Michelle Windsor is a writer who lives north of Boston, Massachusetts, with her husband and two teenage boys. She writes steamy contemporary romance, has achieved Amazon and Barnes & Noble International Best Seller status, and was awarded the Best Contemporary Romance Writer by Passionate Plume Ink in 2019. When Michelle isn't working on another book, you can find her spending time with her family, her German Shepherd, Roman, or enjoying cocktails with her close-knit girlfriends.

You can find out more about Michelle, on her webpage:
www.authormichellewindsor.com